PUFFIN BOOKS

BURGLAR BELLS

In horror, Bernie and Lee watch a man climbing through the window of an empty house in Wood-kirk Avenue. Is he a burglar?

When news breaks out of a burglary in that very same road, Bernie and Lee are convinced that it was the man they saw. They are horrified to find that the description of this man exactly fits that of Mr Herring, the man who is going to marry Miss Daisy, the school secretary.

What should they do? How can they find out for certain if Mr Herring is the burglar? Should they tell Miss Daisy?

Burglar Bells

John Escott

Illustrated by Maureen Bradley

PUFFIN BOOKS

Puffin Books, Penguin Books Ltd, Harmondsworth, Middlesex, England
Viking Penguin Inc., 40 West 23rd Street, New York, New York 10010, U.S.A.
Penguin Books Australia Ltd, Ringwood, Victoria, Australia
Penguin Books Canada Limited, 2801 John Street, Markham, Ontario, Canada L3R 1B4
Penguin Books (N.Z.) Ltd, 182–190 Wairau Road, Auckland 10, New Zealand

First published by Hamish Hamilton Children's Books, 1983
Published in Puffin Books 1986
Copyright © John Escott, 1983
Illustrations copyright © Hamish Hamilton Ltd, 1983
All rights reserved

Printed and bound in Great Britain by
Cox & Wyman Ltd, Reading

Chapter 1

Shocks and Surprises

THE MAN was definitely trying to climb in the window.

Bernie stopped at the end of the driveway and nudged Lee. "That man!" Bernie said. "Look!"

Lee looked, surprise slowly spreading over his face. "He's – he's climbing in the window!"

"I know he's climbing in the window, stupid! I can see that, can't I? I don't need glasses." Bernie had unconsciously taken a few steps back as though what he was observing might in some way be dangerous for him. "Come on, let's get going."

He made a move to hurry along

Woodkirk Avenue. Lee's hand stopped
him.

"Hang on, if he's a burglar – " Lee
began.

8

"If he's a burglar," Bernie said, "I'd just as soon not meet him."

He stopped all the same, fascinated by the scrambling legs as they tried to find a foothold in the wall of the house. It was a large house, like all the others in Woodkirk Avenue, some of which had gardens like small parks, and gate-posts as thick as tree-trunks.

Suddenly, the man slipped and fell backwards.

"Aaah!"

The figure vanished into a tangle of shrubs and bushes which crouched beneath the narrow side window where he had been trying to enter.

"Let's *go*," Bernie said, but Lee was already moving up the drive. Reluctantly, Bernie followed his friend.

The man looked surprised to see them, his head appearing between the

9

greenery. "Oh – ah, yes." He gave a
little laugh, pushing his hair back from
his face. There was a red scratch above
his right eyebrow where one of the

shrubs had attacked him. He stuck out a hand towards Lee. "Uh – could you pull me out, do you think?"

Lee extended a hand and heaved the man on to the path.

"Thank you." The man dusted down the trousers of his dark grey suit, now streaked with green. "I fell."

The two boys stared at him, saying nothing. He seemed remarkably calm for a burglar who'd been caught in the act, Bernie thought. He'd half expected the man to make a run for it.

He was a small man with thinning hair which he kept smoothing into place. At the left side of his nose was a small mark, the shape of a wishbone. Bernie looked at it with interest.

"I forgot the key," the man said suddenly, looking from one boy to the other. "That's why I was trying to get

in through the window. Actually, it was rather careless of me to leave it open, after all you can't be too careful these days, can you? Burglars, I mean."

The boys continued to watch him without speaking. Lee shuffled from foot to foot.

The man looked at Bernie, then at the window. "Look, you wouldn't help me out, would you? I mean, even though I'm not large I'm a bit big for that small window, whereas you look as though you'd pop through easily."

"Me?" Bernie was astonished. "What – what climb through that window?"

"It's perfectly safe," the man assured him. "There's a table the other side you can climb on to. Just be careful not to knock off the potted plant. Then you can open the front door and let me in." He smiled reassuringly. "There are some apples in the kitchen – I bought them yesterday – and you could each have one for helping me."

Apples. Tables with plants on. Would burglars know about such things before they broke into a house? Bernie didn't think they would. He glanced at Lee who was now looking much more relaxed.

Lee shrugged. "I could give you a

bunk up," he told Bernie, as if to say, It's all right, this bloke's no burglar.

They made it look easy, Lee using his shoulder to shove Bernie up to the little window. Bernie stuck his arm through the gap and unfastened the catch. Seconds later, he was jumping down from the table and grabbing the potted plant before it wobbled onto the floor.

The hall was large and dim and smelled like a greenhouse. This, Bernie decided, was due to the variety of plants which sat in tubs and bowls in almost every conceivable place.

"The bloke's a plant freak," Bernie muttered to himself. He went across and undid the Yale lock on the front door. Daylight spread around his feet.

"Splendid," the man said. "Come on, I'll see about those apples." And he walked unhesitatingly across the hall to the kitchen where, sure enough, in the centre of a pine table, stood a bowl of apples and bananas.

"Burglar!" Bernie threw the apple core over a hedge and ran.

Lee chased after him. They were out of Woodkirk Avenue now, running down the alleyway beside Woodkirk

Common. "You thought he was too!"

The man had thanked them again and watched them go down the drive before going back into the house. (In a hurry to get them off the premises? Bernie wondered, then dismissed the thought. It was silly to be suspicious of every little thing.)

In a way, it had been a bit of a let-down. He had imagined a picture of himself in the evening paper. A headline: SCHOOLBOY FOILS BURGLAR. Being interviewed on local radio.

At the time that Bernie was climbing through the window of the house in Woodkirk Avenue, Rosemary Page was screwing up her face in pain in the school secretary's office.

"Hang on, Rosemary," Miss Daisy

told her. "Be brave and suck hard."

Rosemary sucked hard. On an extra-strong mint. One of the ones Miss Daisy kept in a jar in her desk and doled out to injured and unhappy children as needs demanded. For cuts and scratches – plasters and peppermints. For bumps and bruises – witch-hazel and wine gums.

Strong as they were, the peppermints couldn't deaden the sting of the anti-septic cream on Rosemary's elbow.

"There," Miss Daisy said, rolling down the sleeve of Rosemary's shirt. "That'll hold it. I thought it was netball you played, not rugby football."

Rosemary smiled through gritted teeth. She had stayed after school for netball practice and suffered her injury doing a head-over-heels after tripping over the netball post.

"Never mind, it'll be better in no time," Miss Daisy, the eternal optimist, had said.

Everybody called the school secretary 'Miss Daisy' because she had an unpronounceable last name. Her real name was Polish, with z's and w's scattered throughout it. So she was 'Miss Daisy' to one and all.

"Don't forget your school bag," Miss Daisy said, and picked it up off her desk. She tossed it to Rosemary who started to put out a hand to catch it when the sting in her elbow stopped her.

"Ow!"

The bag fell to the floor, half the contents spilling out.

"Oh, I'm sorry, love," Miss Daisy said. "I wasn't thinking. Here, let me pick up your things – oh? What's this?"

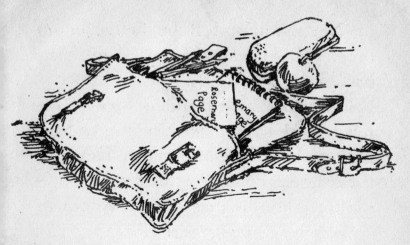

She held a small brown case in her hand.

Rosemary felt her face burning and a sudden tightness in her chest.

Miss Daisy didn't look at Rosemary but continued to gather up the contents of the bag. "I didn't know you wore glasses, love. I hadn't noticed them before."

And Miss Daisy noticed *everything* that went on in Oakhouse Primary School, everybody knew that.

"It – it's a secret," Rosemary said quietly, then realised how stupid that sounded.

Miss Daisy just nodded, going back to her desk to sit down, the brown case in her hand. She was a big woman with a round, kindly face.

"A secret," Miss Daisy repeated. "Well, we all have secrets."

There was a short pause, Rosemary's eyes on the case.

"Even I have a secret," Miss Daisy said at last, as though having considered and made up her mind about something. "Tell you what, we'll make a bargain. You announce your secret tomorrow – and you can announce mine as well."

Rosemary swallowed several times but didn't answer.

"My secret's much bigger than yours

and I hadn't planned to mention it for a while." Miss Daisy got up and came round to Rosemary again. She put a hand on her shoulder. "Only Mr Keane knows about it at school."

Mr Keane was the headmaster. He knew almost as much about what went on in the school as Miss Daisy. Almost, but not quite.

"I – I don't know," Rosemary said. Wearing glasses in front of everybody seemed an enormous price to pay for learning Miss Daisy's secret.

"Is this the first day you've brought them? I expect you planned to put them on this morning but then decided to keep it a secret a bit longer."

"Well –" It was amazing the way Miss Daisy could always put her finger on the truth.

Miss Daisy nodded. "Perfectly under-

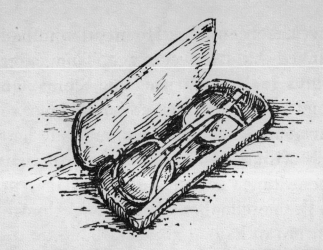

standable. But your secret, like mine, will have to come out sometime."

It was true, of course, Rosemary knew it was. Knew it, yet didn't want to admit it. All day, the glasses had stayed in her school bag, pushed to the bottom. Yet she had been as conscious of them as if they'd been burning a hole in the plastic. "Make sure you wear them at school," her mother had said. "No more squinting at the blackboard."

24

It had been Miss Heywood who had noticed that two weeks ago. Then, after school one day, she had come up quietly to Rosemary and handed her an envelope. "For your mother," she had said with a smile. "Nothing to worry about."

The note had contained a suggestion that Mrs Page took her daughter to have her eyes tested as Rosemary appeared to have difficulty reading the blackboard from the back of the classroom. Later, a trip to the optician had resulted in the gold-framed glasses which Miss Daisy now inspected, having taken them from the case.

"Oh, but they're *lovely*, Rosemary." And she popped them on the girl's nose before Rosemary could stop her. "And they suit you a *treat*."

Rosemary's face burned again.

25

"When do you have to wear them, love? Just in class?"

Rosemary nodded – and was surprised the glasses stayed put. "And watching TV, looking at things in the distance, that sort of thing."

"Well, make sure you wear them tomorrow, love. All right?"

Rosemary shrugged. "All right." There seemed to be no other option.

Miss Daisy went to her desk and opened a drawer. "Now for my secret."

Rosemary was suddenly curious. That Miss Daisy could have a secret at all was astonishing. She was the sort of person who always bursted to tell everybody about everything.

"There!" Miss Daisy held out something.

It was a photograph, the size of a postcard, and it showed the head and shoulders of a man.

"Oh," Rosemary said, not sure what was expected of her.

Miss Daisy laughed. "That is Reggie – Mr Herring – and he and I are going to be married in just three weeks time!"

Rosemary stared at the photograph, then looked up at Miss Daisy and smiled. "Oh," she said, and they both laughed.

Miss Daisy suddenly looked embarrassed. "I know what you're thinking. 'Fancy Miss Daisy getting married at her age.' Well, fifty-four is not old, do you hear? Not old at all."

"Oh, it's not," Rosemary agreed hastily. "And I really am pleased."

It was just that it was such a surprise. For years, Miss Daisy had lived with her elderly mother in a tiny bungalow and, as far as Rosemary knew, the old lady was still alive.

"Reggie has quite a large house," Miss Daisy said as though reading Rosemary's thoughts. "Mother will have two rooms to herself. Reggie's a widower, you see. His wife died four years ago."

Rosemary looked back at the man in the picture. He looked nice enough, although his hair was thinning and there was a little mark beside his nose. It was shaped like a wishbone.

"Where does he live?" Rosemary asked.

"Crosby Road," Miss Daisy said. "He has a house in Crosby Road."

The following morning, as Bernie ate his breakfast, he received some news which made him choke over his toast. It came over the local radio and Bernie only caught the tail end of the report. It was more than enough.

" . . . *and several items of jewellery were taken besides cash. The robbery took place sometime yesterday afternoon when the house, in Woodkirk Avenue, was empty.*

"*Plans for the new town bypass were*

discussed again yesterday . . . "

'I helped a burglar!' Bernie thought.
'I let him into somebody's house!' He
left the rest of his toast to get cold, his
appetite gone.

Chapter 2

Secrets

"THEY'RE NICE," Emma Bates said.

"Pretty," Suzy Yeung told her.

"Better than my glasses," Mervyn Fry said.

Rosemary sat and squirmed.

April Carpenter sniffed. "I may have to wear glasses," she said. Nobody believed her. April just hated not being the centre of attention.

"I wish you'd all stop *staring* at me," Rosemary wailed. "As though I'd suddenly got two heads!"

She took the glasses off and put them on the desk. Ian Kenning immediately snatched them up and put them on. He perched them on the end of his nose like

the Wise Owl in some children's story. Even Rosemary had to laugh.

"Give them back," she said, and held out a hand. "Give them back or I shan't tell you."

"Tell me what?" Ian said.

"A secret," Rosemary said.

So far, she hadn't repeated Miss Daisy's news to anybody, although the school secretary had given her permission to do so. The others had been moving away but the word 'secret' drew them back like pins to a magnet. Even Lee and Bernie who had been discussing something in urgent whispers at the other end of the room looked up.

"What secret? What about?" April couldn't bear other people to know something she didn't.

"Come on, Rosemary, tell us," Mervyn said, perching on the edge of her desk.

"Not until he gives them back," Rosemary said.

Reluctantly, Ian passed the glasses to Rosemary. "So what's the secret?"

"Miss Daisy's getting married," she announced, and saw eyebrows shoot up and eyes pop open. It was one way of taking their minds off her new glasses, she thought, then suddenly realised that this was probably what Miss Daisy had intended. Dear old Miss Daisy. Dear *young* Miss Daisy, Rosemary silently corrected herself.

"What!"

"Miss Daisy – !"

"Getting *married*?"

"Who to?"

"A Mr Herring," Rosemary told them. "He's about the same age as her, I should think. I saw a photograph of him. He's a widower and he lives in Crosby Road."

"When did you find all this out?" April snapped.

"After netball yesterday, when I went to have my elbow patched up."

"Here comes the bride, all fat and wide," sang Ian.

"Shh! Don't be unkind," Rosemary said.

Ian laughed. "Miss Daisy wouldn't mind. She's always making fun of herself."

"I wonder if she'll stop being school secretary when she's married," Mervyn said.

A hush came over them as they thought about this. Rosemary stared out of the window, looking down at the playground. The school had three floors and Miss Heywood's class was on the middle floor.

"I don't know," she said at last. "Oh, I hope not."

"What's he like?" Mervyn asked.

"I told you, he's not very big – "

Ian laughed again. "He'll look funny up against Miss Daisy then. Can you imagine them standing side by side in church?"

"Chapel," Emma corrected him. "Miss Daisy goes to the chapel in Pinner Avenue. Is he nice looking, Rosemary?"

"Sort of. It was hard to tell from the photograph. He had this funny mark by his nose."

"What funny mark?" Lee said from the other end of the classroom. He and

36

Bernie had stopped talking to listen to Rosemary's news.

Rosemary shrugged. "A sort of scar, I suppose."

"A scar!" April shrieked. "Crikey!"

"Not that sort of scar," Rosemary said. "Nothing horrible. Just a little mark by his nose. Shaped like a wishbone."

"What?" Bernie said sharply. He looked at Lee and they both came across to the others. "By his nose?"

"Yes, why?"

"*Where* did you say he lived?" Bernie went on. "Was it Woodkirk Avenue?"

Rosemary frowned. "Woodkirk Avenue? I didn't say anything about Woodkirk Avenue. I told you, he has a house in Crosby Road." She looked from Lee to Bernie, then back to Lee again. "What's the matter?"

"Nothing," Bernie said quickly.

"Nothing at all," Lee said.

And at that moment, Miss Heywood came in and the group broke up.

"Good morning, everybody," Miss Heywood said. She glanced at Rosemary, smiled and raised here eyebrows as she noticed the new glasses, but said nothing. "Come on," she told Bernie and Lee. "You'll have to wait until break to finish your discussion, unless you'd like to tell us all about it."

"Er – no," Bernie said.

"Lots of people have scars," Lee said.

"Not like wishbones they don't," Bernie said. "It *has* to be the same bloke."

It was breaktime and they were under the oak tree by the gates. The shrieks and scuffles about them went

unheeded. There were more important matters to be discussed.

"We could be sure if we saw the photograph Miss Daisy showed Rosemary," Bernie said. "I'll bet she keeps it in her office."

Lee looked alarmed. "What about it?"

Bernie glanced around. "Might be able to get a look after school."

"No," Lee said quickly. "Miss Daisy always locks her office when she goes home. Besides, we have handbell practice tonight, remember?"

Miss Heywood rehearsed the school handbell group on Tuesday and Friday afternoons. Today was Tuesday and they were practising for a concert at an old people's home the following Saturday afternoon.

"We could nip into the office beforehand," Bernie said. "She always takes letters for Mr Keane to sign and her office is empty then."

"You don't know where she keeps the photograph," Lee said.

"Bet you anything it's in the drawer with the peppermints and things."

Lee looked worried. "It's not really our business."

Bernie looked amazed. "What's the matter with you? If it's the same bloke, it means he's a burglar! And I'll bet Miss Daisy doesn't know *that*."

"He might have two houses," Lee said.

"Elephants might fly!" Bernie said. "He was breaking in, that's what he was doing. It was on the radio, I told you."

"Perhaps we should tell the police," Lee said.

Bernie gave him a disgusted glare. "Don't be stupid. We *helped* him, remember? We'd be in dead trouble."

A bell signalled the end of break and the children moved towards the school building. The March sunshine went behind a cloud and a gust of wind ruffled the leaves above Bernie's head.

"Are you going to help or aren't you?"

Lee sighed. "I s'pose so. What do we do if it is him?"

"I don't know," Bernie said. "I wish I did."

Chapter 3

What to do?

TO BERNIE the day seemed endless. By four o'clock his skin prickled with nervous sweat and he had a breathless feeling that seemed to be squeezing the air from his body.

The secretary's office was right next door to Miss Heywood's classroom which, in some ways, made it more difficult as Miss Heywood was in no rush to leave. She knew she had handbell practice to take and wanted to allow the group time to get themselves downstairs to the hall and sort themselves out before she joined the. Bernie and Lee, on the other hand, wanted her safely out of the way before they acted.

43

"Ah, Bernie," Miss Heywood said, seeing them hovering at the back of the classroom. "Will you and Lee fetch the bells and take them down to the hall? You know where they are."

"Uh – well," Bernie began.

"What's the matter? They aren't too heavy for you, I hope."

"No, Miss," Bernie said, and he and Lee went to the cupboard in the corner. It was almost a small room really, shelves of stationery lining the walls and a travelling bag with sixteen hand-bells inside sitting on the floor.

"Miss Daisy will be going to Mr Keane's room any minute," Lee whispered.

"I know that, don't I?" Bernie growled back. "Give me a hand."

Lee grabbed one handle and the two boys hurried out and sprinted down to

44

the hall. Already, most of the other members of the handbell group had arrived.

"Where are you two off?" April asked as the two boys dumped the bag and made for the doorway again.

"Back in a minute!" Bernie called.

They met Miss Heywood coming down the stairs.

"Forgotten something, Miss," Lee said.

"Won't be a jiffy," Bernie assured her.

They had an agonising wait of over two minutes, hiding in Miss Heywood's classroom, before Miss Daisy made her way to Mr Keane's room at the end of the landing.

"Now!" Bernie whispered.

He shot into Miss Daisy's office as though released from a catapult. Lee hovered by the doorway, staring fearfully at the headmaster's room.

"Hurry up!"

"I'm hurrying, aren't I?" Bernie told him. "Here it is, what did I tell you? She keeps everything in this drawer."

"Never mind that, is it him or isn't it?"

Bernie scuttled across. "See for your-self." He held out the photograph.

"It's him," Lee breathed. "Crikey!"

Bernie hurried back to the desk and replaced the picture.

"Let's get out of here."

They made for the stairway where, already, the clear mellow sounds of handbells drifted up to meet them.

They were finishing off *Greensleeves* when Miss Daisy's head appeared round the hall doorway. She waited until the last note died away then clapped her hands. "Lovely. The old folks will be delighted."

Miss Heywood smiled. "It's coming on, isn't it?"

"Oh, it is," Miss Daisy said. "I love the sound of handbells."

"It'll be wedding bells you'll be

hearing soon, I gather," Miss Heywood said. "Rosemary has told us the news. Congratulations."

The children gave a small cheer and Miss Daisy's face turned a delicate shade of pink. "Thank you very much." She looked at the hall clock. "I have to go. I'm meeting Reggie – uh, I mean Mr Herring." She gave a little giggle and disappeared round the doorway.

Bernie looked at Lee and each knew exactly what the other was thinking. What would poor Miss Daisy do when she learned that she was marrying a burglar?

"My mother knows Mr Herring," Rosemary said. "'Reggie Herring?' she said. 'I knew his wife.' Sometimes I think my mother knows everybody."

Bernie and Lee silently agreed. They

were walking up the steep hill which led away from the school building, Rosemary in between the two boys.

"What's he like, did she say?" Bernie wanted to know.

"She seemed to think he and Miss Daisy would get on fine." She had taken off her glasses after coming out of school and her face felt peculiar without them.

"What does he do?" Lee asked.

"Do?"

"For a living," Bernie prompted, impatient and uneasy at the same time.

Rosemary shrugged. "She didn't say. Why?"

"I just wondered, didn't I?" Bernie snapped.

"What's the matter with you?" Rosemary narrowed her eyes. "And what was all that stuff about Woodkirk

Avenue earlier? What made you think
he lived there?"

"Nothing." Bernie glanced at Lee.
"I was mixing him up with somebody
else."

They walked in silence until they were
at the brow of the hill and could look
down across the golf course. The wind
had picked up and low banks of cloud

scudded across the tops of swaying trees.

Rosemary turned up her coat collar. "Woodkirk Avenue? Wait a minute, wasn't that where the burglary was? The one on the local radio news this morning?"

Bernie and Lee said nothing.

Rosemary went on. "The police said it was the latest in a number of similar robberies in the town. They think the same person's doing them all."

Still the boys said nothing and Rosemary stopped walking. She saw them glance nervously at one another.

"What *is* it? Come on, I know there's something. To do with Mr Herring?" Rosemary frowned. "Mr Herring and Woodkirk Avenue and – " She stopped abruptly, her eyes widening. Her voice dropped to a whisper. "And the *burglary*?"

Lee looked at Bernie. "We'll have to tell her. She'll only go on fishing around until she finds out."

"Tell me what?"

"Besides," Lee went on. "We have to do something, if only for Miss Daisy."

"What's Miss Daisy got to do with it?" Rosemary said.

Bernie took a deep breath. "She's marrying a burglar, that's what she's got to do with it."

Silence. Except for the thumping of Rosemary's heartbeat in her own ears.

"How do you know?" she said at last.

And then Bernie and Lee, each telling a little bit of the story, related the events of the previous afternoon and finally how they had seen the photograph in Miss Daisy's desk before the handbell practice.

"You're absolutely certain it's the

same man?" Rosemary said. She had listened without interrupting.

"No doubt about it," Lee told her.

Rosemary thought of Miss Daisy's beaming face the afternoon before when she'd announced her secret. Dear, kind Miss Daisy. It would be dreadful to spoil her happiness, but it would be even worse to let her go ahead and marry a burglar without realising it.

"We mustn't tell another soul," Rosemary said. "Not for the moment, anyway. Not until we've thought of something to do."

"Just let him get on and rob a few more houses, you mean," Bernie said.

"No – well – oh, I don't know. We could watch him, see if he does anything suspicious. I'll try and find out what he does for a living, his real job I mean."

Rosemary lived round the corner from Crosby Road. She wondered which house was Mr Herring's. Her mother would know, and she'd know about the job.

"I suppose we could keep an eye on him at that," Bernie said, warming to the idea of playing detective. "After school. Make sure he's home where he's supposed to be. Maybe catch him nipping out to do a bit of breaking and entering. Follow him, catch him red-handed, and . . . "

"And what?" Lee said.

Neither Rosemary or Bernie had an answer to that.

Chapter 4

Rosemary's Idea

OVER THE NEXT day or so, they learned several things.

Rosemary discovered from her mother that Mr Herring lived in the big, grey-stoned house on the corner of

Crosby Road. She also found out that he used to work for a large company as an accountant but had lost his job a year ago when they cut down on their staff. Now, her mother said, he worked from home, doing accounts for small business people – shops and hair-dressers and plumbers and the like.

"Be easy then, wouldn't it?" Bernie said when Rosemary told the boys.

"How do you mean?" she said.

"Well, working from home, you can nip out anytime, do a bit of burglaring, nip back again. Nobody to ask, 'Hey, where are you off?' "

"According to the evening paper, the robberies all seem to happen during the afternoon," Lee put in.

"More or less the time we bumped into him on Monday," Bernie said, nodding.

He had discovered the name of the people who owned the house in Woodkirk Avenue where he had climbed through the window. Bernie had a friend – a Mrs Stanway – who lived in Woodkirk Avenue. She was always pleased to see him.

"A Mr and Mrs Ashby live at number seven," she had told Bernie. "Why did you want to know?"

"Oh, I – I just wondered," Bernie had said. He hadn't told her about the burglary. He knew she didn't listen to the local radio, nor did she take a newspaper. Mrs Stanway tended to live in a world of her own and Bernie had no intention of alarming her by talking about burglaries just a few houses away from her own front gate. And her husband, Mr Stanway, spent almost all day reading books about history, and he wouldn't want to know either, Bernie decided.

It was strange, he thought, how when you came to like somebody you tried to protect them from things – especially old people. Almost as though they were young children.

Anyway, he'd found out what he wanted to know. The house definitely didn't belong to Mr Reginald Herring. He hadn't bought it as a surprise wedding present for his new bride – at least, not as far as Mrs Stanway knew.

But he *had* been trying to get through the window, and that was the sort of thing burglars did.

And yet he seemed to lead a blameless sort of life.

On Thursday afternoon, after school, Bernie and Lee followed him down to the newsagent's shop in Duke Street where he spent a long time in the room at the back talking to the owner. He had been carrying a briefcase and it seemed he was doing the newsagent's accounts books, just like Rosemary's mother said he did.

On Friday, Miss Daisy didn't turn up at school due to a heavy cold. At half-past four that afternoon, Bernie, Lee and Rosemary followed Mr Herring to Miss Daisy's house after he'd stopped off at a supermarket to buy a bottle of black-currant cordial.

"For her cold," Rosemary said as they stood and shivered in the road. At this rate, they'd all be needing black-currant cordial.

Soon after, he went straight home.

A collection was made at the school and a wedding present – a large barometer inscribed: From all the pupils at

Oakhouse Primary School – was bought for Miss Daisy. Mr Keane delivered it to Mr Herring's house on Saturday morning. All presents, Miss Daisy said, were being kept at her future husband's house as there was more room. Also, it was where they'd be living shortly.

Mr Keane was unaware of three pairs of eyes watching him go up the path to make the delivery, then come back through the swing gate into the road.

"You don't think he's going to run away with all the presents the day before they're going to be married, do you?" Lee said. They were standing behind the hedge which ran along the front of the garden.

"Mr Herring?" Bernie said. "I wouldn't put it past him."

"But that would be *terrible*," Rosemary said.

For the early part of Saturday afternoon, they had to abandon their observation of Mr Herring's house in

order to play with the handbell group at the old people's home. The concert was being held in honour of one of the residents – a lady who'd just had her hundredth birthday. The lady, in her younger days, had herself played hand-bells and loved to hear them. Knowing this, the matron of the home had asked Miss Heywood if her group would come.

They had a marvellous time. All the old people had sung along with all the tunes the group played and everybody clapped loudly at the end.

It was gone four o'clock when they finally left, although Miss Heywood had rushed off ten minutes before to catch a train as she was going away for the weekend.

Mr Page picked up Rosemary, collec-ting the bells as well. It had been arranged that Rosemary's father would keep the bells over the weekend as Miss Heywood didn't have time to take them back to the school.

Bernie and Lee went with Rosemary in the car, neither of them explaining that the reason they were cadging a lift was to get to Mr Herring's house as quickly as possible.

As Bernie had said earlier, "With Miss Daisy laid up with a cold and no accounts work for Mr Herring to do, Saturday afternoon might be just the time for a burglary."

Lee had agreed. "Lots of people go out on Saturdays. There are empty houses everywhere."

Rosemary was less certain about this but didn't say so. Perhaps they would be too late. Perhaps Mr Herring would have gone out already.

But he hadn't. They saw this as they went by in Mr Page's car. Mr Herring was in his garden, tying a climbing rose tree to some trellis-work outside the front room window.

Mr Page took the handbells indoors while Rosemary and the two boys went back round the corner to Crosby Road.

"We can't hang around his gate when he's in the garden," Lee said. "Especially Bernie and me, he might remember our faces."

"So how are we going to know if he goes out?" Bernie said.

They thought about this for a minute and it was Rosemary who came up with the answer. Rosemary could always cook up a home-made device to suit the occasion.

"Wait here," she told them and ran back home.

A few minutes later she returned with a large handbell and a length of hairy string.

"Now what?" Lee said.

"A sort of signal," Rosemary told them.

Bernie frowned. His imagination didn't run to such things.

"I'll show you," Rosemary said. And she did.

It was a simple idea, but effective. The end of the ball of string was tied to the handbell's leather strap. Lee was left holding the bell, sitting in the bus shelter around the corner from Mr Herring's house. Rosemary and Bernie walked round to Mr Herring's gate, unravelling the string behind them. They stayed close to the high hedge so as not to be seen. Then Bernie cut off the string with his penknife and, when

Mr Herring was occupied with a very tricky bit of rose-staking, Rosemary tied the end of the string to the bottom of his swing gate. There was a strong spring on the gate so that it automatically closed behind whoever went in or out.

Making sure the unwound length of string was well concealed under the hedge along the front of the garden, Rosemary and Bernie went back to the bus shelter.

"Done," she told Lee. "Now we just keep the string taut and if that gate is opened or closed we shall know about it."

"Because the bell will ring," Lee nodded. "Clever Rosie."

Bernie said nothing, annoyed that he never had ideas like that.

Several people went by.

A woman looked curiously at the bell but didn't stop. A young man in a leather jacket asked them if they were waiting for somebody to give them a ring, then went off chuckling at his own joke. Three younger children stopped and stared at the bell until Bernie chased them off.

At five o'clock, just as the three of them were getting fed up and Lee was about to suggest they sneaked round and made sure Mr Herring hadn't gone out some other way – the bell rang in his lap.

In fact, it not only rang it fell on to the pavement and rolled across into the gutter.

"He's going out!" Bernie said, leaping up.

They rushed round the corner just in

time to see Mr Herring walking in the
opposite direction. He was carrying a
small shopping bag.

"Burglar's tools!" Bernie whispered.

"What about the bell?" Lee said.
"We can't just leave it."

"If we hang about, he'll be gone," Bernie said. He looked at Rosemary. "You see to it while Lee and I follow him."

Rosemary started to protest but they were already halfway down Crosby Road after the retreating figure of Mr Herring.

"If you hurry, you could catch us up," Lee called back.

Rosemary stamped back to the bus shelter. That was the trouble with having good ideas, you were left to clear them up! Catch them up! Fat chance of that. She sat down in the shelter and said a rude word. Then she sat and scowled for a full five minutes.

And then the bell rang again.

Rosemary jumped. It was still in the gutter but had been jerked into a different position.

Somebody had gone in or out of Mr Herring's gate.

She rushed across, scooped up the bell, then ran round into Crosby Road. An empty road.

73

Had Mr Herring come back again? If so, where were Bernie and Lee? There was the string, still tied to the gate. It looped behind her as she approached with caution.

The garden was empty. Rosemary hesitated, then pushed the gate and

went up the path, a hollow feeling in the pit of her stomach.

The house stood silent, the climbing rose now neatly pinned to the trellis. At one side a path led around the building to a side gate. The gate was open.

Rosemary hesitated again, but only for a second.

Chapter 5

Run for it!

BERNIE AND LEE hung around outside the supermarket in Duke Street.

"Shopping!" Bernie said disgustedly.

"Well, he was carrying a shopping bag," Lee reminded him. He grinned. "Perhaps he's putting the groceries on top of his burglar's tools."

"Oh, very funny," Bernie growled.

"He's coming out, anyway," Lee said.

And Mr Herring emerged from the supermarket, his shopping bag now bulging with packages.

"I can't see him taking that lot with him when he goes breaking and entering, can you?" Lee said. They watched

Mr Herring's reflection in a shop window to avoid being seen. "Be a bit of a nuisance."

"All right, all right," Bernie snapped.

Mr Herring used the pelican crossing to go over the road. Bernie and Lee followed some way behind amongst other shoppers.

"He's going home again," Lee said. "Well, that was a waste of time."

"Might as well follow and make sure," Bernie said, disappointment in his voice.

"Perhaps he'll stop off and rob a bank on the way," Lee said.

Bernie aimed a kick at him but Lee dodged out of the way.

Rosemary went round to the back of the building. A narrow garden, shaped like a V, stretched away to a tall fence, beyond which were the houses in the street behind.

At the back of Mr Herring's house, a lean-to conservatory with a plastic corrugated roof sloped away from the wall. A window in the conservatory was wide open. Too wide for a cool March evening.

Rosemary could hear movement inside the building, a shuffling sound and the soft thud of something being dropped or knocked over. She looked through the window. The sounds seemed to be coming from upstairs.

Go and get somebody, that was the sensible thing to do. Rosemary told herself she'd do just that – after she'd had a quick peep inside.

She was surprised to find that she was still holding the bell, the length of

string trailing to the swing gate where it was still tied. Most of the slack had been used up and, after she'd climbed on to the window-ledge, Rosemary popped the bell into the plastic guttering above her, leaving her hands free to swing herself through into the conservatory.

French windows led through into the house via what was obviously the living room. An ancient television in a cabinet stood in one corner and a jumble of books were crammed into shelving above. Heavy furniture with floral-patterned covers was pushed haphazardly against walls, and a dark oak table was covered in books and papers, columns of neatly written figures filling the pages.

The sounds continued to come from upstairs.

It would be the bravest thing she had ever done, Rosemary told herself (*And the silliest*, a little voice inside her said, but she pretended not to hear it.) She just *had* to know.

The hallway was large and dim, dark-stained panels and plum-red carpet. A small table with a telephone on it stood under the stairs. These were steep and, as she climbed, Rosemary was certain there would be at least one that creaked.

But she got to the top without making a sound. And there was no need to go any farther.

Along the landing was a small room, and in it she could see the back of a man. He was stooping over a black plastic bag, the sort Rosemary's father used for garden rubbish. The man was wearing jeans and a leather jacket and

Rosemary suddenly realised it was the same man who had passed them earlier and made the joke about them waiting for a ring.

He was putting things into the plastic bag and it was then that Rosemary caught a glimpse of Miss Daisy's barometer. *'He's stealing her wedding presents!'* she thought, and a tidal wave of anger swept through her.

Before she had been afraid, now she was just *furious*. 'Get help,' she thought. 'Get the police!'

Quickly and quietly, she padded back downstairs to where the telephone stood on the table. After an anxious glance back up the stairs she lifted the receiver, wincing at the 'ping'.

Shaking fingers dialled 999. Rosemary couldn't believe they were her own.

The boys turned into Crosby Road, Mr Herring some way ahead of them.

"Rosemary's probably gone home," Bernie said.

"Do you think so?"

"She was a bit fed up being left behind."

"She needn't have been," Lee said. "She didn't exactly miss any excitement, did she?"

"Do you *have* to go on and on?" Bernie said.

"Sorry," Lee said.

Ahead, Mr Herring was halfway along Crosby Road.

There was another 'ping' as Rosemary replaced the receiver.

And then another, more terrifying sound.

"Hey!"

She whirled around and looked up.
He was standing at the top of the stairs.
"Who the devil – ?"
She didn't wait to hear the rest. Her

feet seemed to take wing as she fled back through the living room and out of the French windows.

"Come back!" he yelled.

But that was the last thing Rosemary intended to do. She was up and over the window ledge and running down the back garden.

The trouble was it only seemed to lead to the fence at the end, and that was too high to climb. She would be trapped!

"Oh!" Rosemary looked desperately over her shoulder.

And there he was, framed in the open conservatory window, half in, half out. He had thrown the black plastic bag out ahead of him. Now, seeing Rosemary crouching amongst the cabbages, he smiled. It wasn't a nice smile.

He began to climb out.

At that precise moment, Mr Herring opened his gate.

The length of hairy string was given a sudden jerk.

Rosemary thought she was seeing things. One moment the man was climbing out of the window, his horrible smiling eyes fixed on her, the next second the large handbell was yanked from the guttering by the trailing string.

It landed squarely on the man's head with a muffled *bo-ng-ng-ng!* He staggered around like a drunkard for a few moments then fell forwards into a bed of cauliflowers.

Rosemary blinked then found herself laughing and crying at the same time, her legs weak with relief.

And then Mr Herring came around the side of the building. The scene brought him to an abrupt halt. He had

followed the piece of hairy string,
totally mystified, expecting anything.
Now he simply looked astonished, his
mouth opening and shutting like his
own swing gate.

And outside that gate, Bernie and Lee arrived at the same moment as a large white police car.

"Crikey!" Bernie said. "How did they get in on it?"

"Maybe he *did* rob a bank after all," Lee said. "When we weren't looking."

"*Something* certainly happened when we weren't looking," Bernie said.

Chapter 6

A LOT OF explanations were needed. Especially to Mr Herring who couldn't for the life of him understand how a handbell had come to be tied by a long piece of string to his front gate.

Rosemary began with that and worked backwards while the two policemen escorted a dazed and bewildered burglar to their car. Bernie and Lee, who had been unable to resist coming round the back of the house to investigate all the activity, added their bit to the story.

Mr Herring stared at them. "But of course, I remember you now. You were the two young men who helped me get into my friend's house."

"Your *friend's house?*" Lee said.

Mr Herring nodded. "John and Katy Ashby's house. I'd been looking after it while they were in Italy – watering all the plants, generally making sure everything was all right." He nodded after the departing burglar. "It seems that young man may be the one the police have been looking for. The one who did the robbery in Woodkirk Avenue last Monday."

"We thought you . . . " Bernie's voice tailed off.

Mr Herring laughed. "You thought *I* was the burglar? I see! Well, you should have checked on the number of the house that was burgled. It was number *eleven* Woodkirk Avenue. You helped me get into number *seven*."

"They didn't give the number on the radio," Bernie said sulkily. "How were we to know?"

"An understandable mistake," Mr Herring said. "After all, it was the same afternoon. The day before my friends returned, as it happens, hence the fruit and groceries I'd got in for them."

The chapel where Miss Daisy and Mr Herring were married had just one bell. And that, as Bernie put it, sounded "like somebody kicking a milk churn."

However, Oakhouse Primary School Handbell Group made sure Miss Daisy had a taste of real wedding bells. They lined up like a guard of honour outside the chapel, ringing peal after tumbling

peal until the chapel grounds were filled with the sound.

A smiling Miss Daisy, tears of happiness in her eyes, and a beaming Mr Herring passed between them.

They were all invited to the reception at the Blue Boar Hotel.

"It's been the happiest day of my life," Miss Daisy told the group. "I can't thank you enough." She looked at Rosemary. "And as for you, Rosemary – well it's only because of you that we have any wedding presents left at all!"

Rosemary went pink. "Don't forget Bernie and Lee," she said.

"And the bell," Bernie added. "Don't forget the bell."

As if anybody could.